Jonathan Coe was born in Birmingham, UK, in 1961. He began writing at an early age. His first surviving story, a detective thriller called *The Castle of Mystery*, was written when he was eight. His first published novel was *The Accidental Woman* in 1987, but it was his fourth, *What a Carve Up!*, which established his reputation as one of England's finest comic novelists, winning the John Llewellyn Rhys Prize in 1985 and being translated into many languages. Seven bestselling novels and many other awards have followed, including the 2005 Samuel Johnson Prize for *Like a Fiery Elephant*, a biography of the experimental novelist, B. S. Johnson. Jonathan Coe lives in London.

Fiction

The Accidental Woman
A Touch of Love
The Dwarves of Death
What a Carve Up!
The House of Sleep
The Rotters' Club
The Closed Circle
The Rain Before It Falls
The Terrible Privacy of Maxwell Sim
Expo 85
Number 11

Short Fiction

Loggerheads and Other Stories

Non-fiction

Like a Fiery Elephant: The Story of B. S. Johnson
Marginal Notes, Doubtful Statements

THE BROKEN MIRROR

A Fable

Jonathan Coe

Illustrated by Chiara Coccorese

Unbound

This edition first published in 2017

Unbound
6th Floor Mutual House, 70 Conduit Street, London W1S 2GF

www.unbound.com

Text Design by Ellipsis

A CIP record for this book is available from the British Library

ISBN 978-1-78352-417-4 (trade hbk)
ISBN 978-1-78352-418-1 (ebook)
ISBN 978-1-78352-419-8 (limited edition)

Printed and bound in China by C&C Offset Printing Co. Ltd

Dear Reader,

The book you are holding came about in a rather different way to most others. It was funded directly by readers through a new website: Unbound. Unbound is the creation of three writers. We started the company because we believed there had to be a better deal for both writers and readers. On the Unbound website, authors share the ideas for the books they want to write directly with readers. If enough of you support the book by pledging for it in advance, we produce a beautifully bound special subscribers' edition and distribute a regular edition and e-book wherever books are sold, in shops and online.

This new way of publishing is actually a very old idea (Samuel Johnson funded his dictionary this way). We're just using the internet to build each writer a network of patrons. Over the page, you'll find the names of all the people who made it happen.

Publishing in this way means readers are no longer just passive consumers of the books they buy, and authors are free to write the books they really want. They get a much fairer return too – half the profits their books generate, rather than a tiny percentage of the cover price.

If you're not yet a subscriber, we hope that you'll want to join our publishing revolution and have your name listed in one of our books in the future. To get you started, here is a £5 discount on your first pledge. Just visit unbound.com, make your pledge and type **mirror5** in the promo code box when you check out.

Thank you for your support,

Dan, Justin and John
Founders, Unbound

SUPPORTERS

Unbound is a new kind of publishing house. Our books are funded directly by readers. This was a very popular idea during the late eighteenth and early nineteenth centuries. Now we have revived it for the internet age. It allows authors to write the books they really want to write and readers to support the books they would most like to see published.

The names listed below are of readers who have pledged their support and made this book happen. If you'd like to join them, visit www.unbound.com.

Pamela Abbott

Alice Adams

Geoff Adams

John Adams

David Adger

Phil Agius

Moose Allain

Sergio Amadori

Robert Andrews

Sandra Armor

Philippe Auclair

Clare Barker

Sophie Barker

Ruby Bastiman

David Belbin

Emma Bell

Daryl Berrell

Jonathan Blackie

Nadia Bouzidi

Joanna Bowen

John Boxall

John Boyne

Richard W H Bray

Jonathan Bridgland

Emma Brown

Nicky Brown

Simon J. Brown

Gareth Buchaillard-Davies

Steven Buckeridge

Freya Bullock

Paul Bussey

John Caley

Jonathan Cole

Stephen Cooper

Elizabeth Harper Cowan

Paul Daintry

Harriet Fear Davies

Remembering Owen Davies

Royce Cerf Dehmer

Rob Delaney

Tasja Dorkofikis

Chris Dottie

Jenny Doughty

John Dunbar

Valerie Duskin

Jez Fielder

Paul Fielder

Julia Fox

Mark Fraser

Babette Gallard

Annabel Gaskell

Mike Gautrey

Jane Gibbs

Ben Golding

Giles Goodland

Tom Goodrich

Lucille Grant

Jason Hares

Sean Harkin

Claire R E Harris

Amanda Hart

Barry Hasler

Andrew Hearse

Barry Hecker

Caroline Hennigan

Patrick Heren

Philip Hewitt

Matthew H. Hill

Greg Hitchcock

Paul Hodgson

Peter Hogan

Janice Holve

Mary Horlock

Jeff Horne

Jacob Howe

Sarah A Hubert

Matthew Iles

Caroline Irby

Rivka Isaacson

Natascha Jaeger

Stephen Jessop & Donna Laurie

Mark Jones

Julia Jordan

Peter Jordan

Ros Kennedy

Dan Kieran

Patrick Kincaid

Mit Lahiri

Basia Lautman

Garth Leder

Bridget Caron Lee

Justin Lewis

Marina Lewycka

Diana Lilley

Rebecca Lovett

Seonaid Mackenzie

Koukla MacLehose

M. J. Magee

Paul Main

Marianthi Makra

Philippa Manasseh

David Manns

Milcah Marcelo

Katrin Mäurich

Tom McDermott

Brigid McDonough

Roy McMillan

Sam McNabb

Jenny Middleton

John Mitchinson

Chris Monk

Mark Muldowney

Linda Nathan

Carlo Navato

Jay Newman

Jules McNally Norman

Ashley Norris

Julia O'Brien

Rodney O'Connor

Catherine O'Flynn

Michele O'Leary

Misha and Marlon Owen

Scott Pack

Rina Palumbo

Janice Parsons

Finley Peake

Tony Peake

Pernilla Pearce

Bianca Pellet

Edward Penning

Sonya Permyakova

Cynda Pierce

Justin Pollard

Lorca and Llara Prado

Rhian Heulwen Price

Dylan & Esme Price-Davey

David Quantick

Julia Raeside

Alice Rees

Paul Rhodes

Rachael Robinson

David Roche

Alun Roderick

Taylor Royle

Anna Sambles

Libby Sambles

Susan Sandon

Tim Saxton

David Sayers

Dean Scott

Dr David A Seager

Alan Searl

John Sheehan

Joanne Sheppard

David Shriver

Caroline Shutter

Harry Simeone

Diane Sinclair

John Skelton

Hazel Slavin

Nicholas Snowdon

Stuart Southall

Loredana Spadola

Ian Spence

Clive Stock

Ewan Tant

Steve Thorp

Jem Thorpe-Woods

Linda Todgers

Graham Tomlinson

Transreal Fiction

Annabel Turpin

Anne Tyley

Despina Vassiliadou

Mark Vent

Paul Vincent

John Wagstaff

Steve Walsh

Jeremy Warmsley

Alan Webster

Alice Wenban-Smith

Elsie Mai Hâf Westmore

Wiz Wharton

Vicki Whittaker

Patrick Wildgust

Mike Williams & Munson the
    Alaskan Malamute

Reuben Willmott

Sarah Wilson

Sophie Wilson

Steve Woodward

AUTHOR'S NOTE

The town in this story is called Kennoway, which is the name of a real town in Fife, Scotland, where my great-great-grandparents used to live. But this story is set somewhere in England, and the real town and the fictional town have got nothing to do with each other.

ONE

Claire was eight years old when she found the mirror. It was raining that day. Not heavy rain, but warm summer rain, with thick, occasional drops, falling from a dull, slate-grey sky. These were the last few days of the school holidays, and the weather had only just changed. They had been lucky this year: the sun had shone for almost the whole of their two weeks away. As usual, Claire and her parents had been to Wales for their holiday, staying in a small rented cottage a few miles from the sea. They had gone to the beach every day and for a short time Claire had forgotten her pervasive sense of loneliness. Towards the end of the holiday she had even made friends with another little girl, a nine-year-old called Lisa who was an only child, just like her. They had promised to keep in touch, but Lisa lived hundreds of miles away so there wasn't really much point. Meanwhile Claire's best friend Aggie was still on holiday somewhere with her mum and dad, so Claire had nobody to play with for the time being.

It had been a lovely two weeks but now, after only one day at home, everybody's mood had changed. As soon as they returned, Claire's father had sat down on the sofa with a pile of unread letters, and after he had finished reading them, he seemed angry with everyone and everything. Now her parents were talking earnestly in the kitchen about something to do with his job, and Claire could think of nothing to do except wander out into the garden. It was a small garden, and it didn't take her long to get bored, out there by herself. She would have played on the swing, but one of the ropes was broken. So instead, she walked down to the bottom of the garden, and slipped out through the hole in the fence, where one of the posts had rotted away.

From here, you could soon reach the rubbish dump. In the distance there rose a modest, grassy hill, dotted with rocks and heather, where Claire's parents would sometimes take her for walks on Sunday afternoons. There was a fantastic view of the whole town from the top. But before you got very far along the path towards this hill, there was a clump of dense, stubbly bushes on the left, and once you had pushed your way through those, the ground fell away at your feet into a sheer slope, like the edge of a cliff. But if you trod carefully, you could scramble down the slope – clutching for support onto the weeds which sprung out of the chalky soil – and that was how you got to the dump.

Claire didn't come here often. This was only the third or fourth time. To be honest, it wasn't a very nice place at all. It was full of big plastic bags with their contents spilling out, sharp pieces of metal which might catch you in the leg if you weren't looking out for them, and rotting items of food

which people had thrown away and which had started to smell terrible. In fact the smell was the worst thing about it.

None the less, there was something about the dump that Claire liked. She felt somehow at home in the company of all these thrown-away things. And just occasionally, you might find something useful. Once she had found a radio here, which she had taken back to her bedroom, and although she had never been able to get it to work, it had looked nice, sitting on the table beside her bed, until her parents had eventually persuaded her to get rid of it and bought her a new one for her birthday. The other thing she wanted for her bedroom was an alarm clock so she wondered if today she might be lucky enough to find one.

Almost immediately, however, something quite different caught her eye. There was a flash of light from the top of one of the rubbish piles and when Claire went over to see what it was, she found a fragment of broken mirror, just a couple of inches wide, but with rough, jagged edges forming a shape like an irregular star. She bent down and picked it up – very gingerly, because she didn't want to cut herself. As she took it in her hand, she was dazzled by the clear, pale blue of the sky reflected on the mirror's surface, and the sudden play of sunlight flung back by the glass as she held it and turned it this way and that. The brightness of the light even hurt her eyes for a moment or two, so that she had to shield them with her arm as she looked down at the mirror.

Holding the mirror cautiously between finger and thumb, Claire scrambled back to the edge of the dump and found a

spot to sit down. Then she laid it flat in her palm and took a closer look Leaning over, she could see the reflection of her own pale, freckly, enquiring face, and beyond that, the blueness of the sky which, the more she looked at it, seemed to be one of the purest and most beautiful colours she had ever seen. She was staring into the depths of the mirror, enjoying the richness of this colour in an almost dreamlike state, when a couple of raindrops fell onto the surface of the glass and startled her out her daydream. She wiped them away with her sleeve and then glanced up at the sky, frowning. How could raindrops be falling from such a blue sky? Except that – and here was the strange thing – now that she looked at it, the sky wasn't blue at all. It was just as grey as it had been when she first left the house: and not just grey, in fact, but mottled over with shifting, fast-moving clouds that were as black as charcoal.

Claire looked again into the mirror lying in the palm of her hand. The same pale, freckly face looked back at her. And behind it was the same blue, cloudless sky. And then she saw something fly through the sky, directly behind her head. It was a huge bird – flying so close above her that she could see the soft texture of its feathers and the beady gleam of its fast, searching eye; so close above her that in an involuntary movement she ducked and covered her head with one arm, afraid that the bird was going to fly into her. But it made no sound; and when she looked up into the sky again a second later, there was nothing there.

TWO

Claire was almost certain that the bird she had seen was an eagle. An eagle was the only bird she could think of that was as large as this one, and whose feathers would send off the same wonderful golden shimmer. But even she (who had very little knowledge of birds) knew that there were no eagles in this part of the country.

She looked up again, and scanned the sky from one end to the other. Where had the eagle gone, in any case? It couldn't have disappeared completely. But try as she might, she could not see it anywhere in the lowering, cloudy sky.

Claire was getting cold now, and was also convinced that it was going to rain very soon. So she put the fragment of mirror carefully into the pocket at the front of her dress, and scrambled up the side of the dump towards the bushes at the top. In a few minutes she had squeezed through the hole in the fence and was back at the bottom of her garden. She had not been away for long: she could still see her mum and dad sitting at the kitchen table, talking to each other and surrounded by papers. Her mum got up and went over to the sink by the window to fill the kettle. She saw Claire and waved. Claire waved back.

Turning away from the house, she took the mirror out of her pocket and looked at it again. Instead of leaning over it, this time, she held it at arm's length, level with her face. At first everything seemed normal but then she looked into it more carefully and noticed something odd about the reflection behind her.

Claire's house was part of an estate on the outskirts of the town, and it had been built about five years ago. All the houses were the same size, the same shape, and were built of the same modern red brick. And sure enough, she *could* see a house – or at least a building – reflected in the mirror, beyond the image of her own face, but it didn't appear to be Claire's house at all. The bricks were much bigger, and were made of much older stone, and were a sandy, yellowy sort of colour. As Claire tilted the mirror in her hand, she could see more of this building: the windows were not square and ugly like theirs, but all sorts of different shapes – arched, round, oval, hexagonal – and they were criss-crossed with metalwork arranged into complex and wonderful patterns. Sunlight glinted back off the windows, dazzling her once again and prompting her seriously to wonder if none of this was real at all, and her eyes were somehow starting to play tricks on her. Maybe this mirror was just a bit dirty: the surface did seem to be streaked with faint marks that wouldn't come off, no matter how hard she rubbed, and Claire supposed that this might account for the way it didn't appear to reflect things properly. And yet, the building she could see behind her own face did seem to be awfully clear. She looked at it again, tilting the mirror further upwards so that she could see higher and higher up the surface of the sandstone walls, right up to the top. The roof, she noticed, was made of tiles that were also yellowish, and there were some flags planted at the crest, rippling in a gentle breeze. (She couldn't make all of them out, but one of them showed a red dragon, against a backdrop of green and white.) Also on the roof was—

And now Claire gasped out loud, and blinked, and rubbed her eyes in disbelief. Because what she saw at the crest of the roof was the strangest thing of all. A row of gigantic seashells.

Claire put down the mirror and whirled around quickly to look back at her house. There it was, as plain and as squat as ever. The very fact that it looked so boring was almost a comfort, at that moment. She gazed at it for quite a while, taking in the solidness, the reality of it, before raising the mirror slowly to the level of her eyes again. She was almost afraid to look into it this time. Then, instead of staring into it directly, she tilted the mirror upwards once more, up to the roof of the strange, massive old building that it appeared to reflect. She adjusted the angle until she had a steady view of the row of seashells. There were about twelve of them, and each one looked big enough for a girl of Claire's age to crawl into and curl up inside. She turned the mirror slowly and carefully, looking closely at each shell, one after the other. She wanted to be sure of something in her mind. A realisation had been creeping over her. When she was quite certain that she wasn't mistaken, she put the mirror away in her pocket, sat down on the damp grass, and started to think.

This is what she was thinking:

Two days ago (was it only two days? It seemed more like two weeks) Claire and Lisa had been playing together on the beach in Wales. For the last day of their holiday, they had decided they were going to do something special, and had started to build a sandcastle. Not just an ordinary sandcastle, but a really spectacular one. They had spent most of the day working on it. The castle they had built was like something out of a fairy tale, complex and higgledy-piggledy, with lots of different courtyards and towers, all set at strange heights and linked by a mazy network of spiral staircases. They had finished by decorating it with flags and seashells. They had bought the flags from the shop by the beach. You got five different flags for a pound. One of them, Claire remembered, was a red dragon on a background of green and white: her dad had explained that it was the national flag of Wales. In the afternoon they had scoured the beach and the nearby rock pools, looking for the most beautiful seashells they could find, and then they had decorated the castle, placing the shells at nicely judged intervals all over the walls, roofs and battlements. It was late in the afternoon when the castle was completed to their satisfaction. Lisa took pictures of it on her smartphone, and Claire's dad took some photos with his camera. They all agreed that it was the most fabulous sandcastle anyone had ever made.

And here it was. Claire was convinced that the building she could see reflected in the mirror was the same castle: only this time it was not built of sand, and it was more than

just a few feet tall. It was made of real stone, and it rose up, proudly and majestically, to a height many times greater than the little houses on Claire's estate. For some reason, though, only the mirror could see it.

Just then, Claire's mother opened the back door and called her in for lunch. Claire rose to her feet and made her way up the garden path. When she was almost at the kitchen door, she lifted her mirror, turned it and looked at the reflection. The door she could see in the mirror was, of course, quite different. It was low and arched, and around the curve of the arch she could see curious writing, and figures of strange animals, carved into the stone.

So now it seemed that Claire was about to find out the answer to a question which had already started to preoccupy her.

What was inside the castle?

THREE

'What are you doing, love?' Claire's mother asked. She was staring at her daughter in some puzzlement, because – instead of sitting down at the kitchen table for her lunch – Claire was standing with her back to it against the far wall, and she was looking intently into what seemed to be a dirty, broken fragment of old mirror.

'Nothing, Mum,' she answered. 'It's just a game that I'm playing.'

'Well hurry up and eat ,' said her mother. 'I don't want it to get cold.'

Claire's dad was already sitting at the table, waiting to start his lunch. His fork was poised over his food, in his left hand. At least, that's what was happening in the real world. In the magical world reflected in Claire's mirror, the picture was slightly different. Her dad was still holding a fork, but it was about ten times its normal size – the size of the trident which Claire had seen in the pictures in one of her schoolbooks, carried by Poseidon, the Greek God of the Sea. The way her dad was holding it made him seem like a king, and this effect

was reinforced by the crown that the mirror showed him to be wearing on his head. It was an unusual – but very beautiful – sort of crown: four big seashells, full of whirls and curlicues and surmounted by a bright red starfish. Her mother was wearing a crown, too: according to the mirror, she still had her hair curlers in place, but behind them was a silver diadem which seemed to be fashioned in the shape of an upturned octopus. This reflection made her look so queenlike and graceful that it was quite a shock to Claire when she heard her mother say in a harsh voice, 'I won't tell you again. Put that filthy thing down and come and eat, won't you? I haven't cooked this just so it can sit on the table all day.'

As if almost in a trance, Claire came to the table and sat down at her usual place, still holding the mirror in front of her eyes. She kept glancing at her parents to see if they had noticed that there was anything strange about it. To her, the reflections it was giving off seemed so bright and dazzling, so different to the muted colours and dull surroundings of the kitchen that she couldn't understand why her mum and dad weren't themselves drawn to it, as surely and irresistibly as all people are drawn to the sparkle of a precious ruby or diamond.

'I told you to put that away,' said her mum, as she spooned potato waffles onto her plate. (In the mirror they looked like pink starfish.)

'But don't you think it's amazing,' said Claire, 'the way it makes everything look different?'

For the first time – but still without looking very interested –

her mum leaned over the mirror and stared closely at it for a few seconds.

'Sorry, love, I can't see what you're talking about,' she said flatly. 'If you want me and your father to join in with your games, you'll have to tell us what the rules are first.'

'She lives in a dream world anyway,' said her father, munching on his food.

Claire sighed, and for the time being gave up on the idea of sharing her discovery with her mum and dad. With a great effort of will she put the mirror face down on the table and started eating. It wasn't much fun trying to snatch glimpses of the reflections while her parents looked on disapprovingly. She would do some proper exploring as soon as the meal was over.

She ate up her lunch as quickly as she could and then left the kitchen and went into the sitting room. She couldn't wait to see what it would look like in the mirror. Here, instead of the flat-screen TV and her parents' boring pictures of landscapes and country scenes, the walls were hung with exquisite tapestries showing enormous whales, leaping dolphins and long, scaly sea-serpents with their bodies entwined around the hulls of ancient ships and galleons. The walls themselves seemed to be about four or five times as high as the walls of Claire's sitting room. At one end there were three arched windows, leading out onto a balcony or terrace, with a balustrade carved out of the same yellow sandstone that the rest of the castle was made of. If you stood and leaned against this balustrade, you would have an incredible view of a vast expanse of sea, a sea almost as flawless in its blueness and stillness as the sky which blended into it on the far horizon.

The infuriating thing was this: Claire couldn't lean against the balustrade and look across at the ocean. She couldn't lean against it because it didn't exist. There was no way of locating it, walking towards it, or touching it. It existed only in the world reflected by this miraculous mirror: a mirror which – she was certain of this by now – somehow managed to reflect not the ordinary, overfamiliar things of which her everyday world consisted, but the things she might dream about – the things that until now would have existed only in her imagination.

Her head swimming with a strange combination of excitement and frustration, Claire now walked upstairs and went into her bedroom. How small and ordinary it seemed after the seaweedy splendours of the royal chambers she had been looking at in the mirror downstairs. Her single bed stood against one wall, with its drab, dark green coverlet; and sitting on top of it, looking back at her with his plaintive, unmoving brown eyes, was her favourite toy – the thing she probably loved most in all the world – a small, fluffy, orange-and-black-striped tiger who many years ago she had decided to call (without too much effort of imagination) Tiger.

Claire held up the mirror to see whether its reflection offered any improvement upon reality.

Again, she could hardly believe what it showed her. Instead of the small, mean little window, looking out over her scrap of back garden, she could once again see an expanse of shimmering turquoise ocean, dappled with sunlight and framed by a shapely arched window which had no glass in it at all. Her bed was transformed into a magnificent four-poster, with the top of each post surmounted by a beautiful wooden carving of a seashell. The flowing, ocean-blue velvet curtains were dotted with a vivid pattern of tiny red, yellow and orange fish. The bank of pillows and cushions stacked up at one end were decorated with the same pattern, and they looked incredibly soft and inviting. In fact Claire would have wanted to throw herself onto the bed in a rapture immediately if she had not been stopped short by the sight of the astonishing creature which appeared to lie stretched out, full-length, on the silky bedclothes. It was an enormous tiger, its flanks covered in soft, long, reddish-golden fur, which Claire could see moving slowly up and down as the superb creature breathed in and out with heavy, sleepy breaths. Its eyes were closed in sleep, but when Claire angled the mirror so that she could look clearly at its face, the animal seemed to sense that it was being watched, because it raised its head and blinked at her and then, instead of growling or snarling in warning, as a wild tiger would probably have done in real life, it rolled over slightly and reached out its paws in a languid, affectionate movement, just like a cat that has been woken from sleep by its owner.

'Oh, you beautiful, beautiful thing,' Claire murmured, staring more and more intently into the mirror, and almost beside herself with frustration that she could not actually reach out to touch the creature and bury her face and hands in its fur.

How could something that she could see so clearly not be real? How could the mirror be showing things that were twice as exciting, a hundred times more magical than the dull, workaday world that was all around her? Claire didn't understand. All she knew was that she had chanced, that day, upon a gift that was rare and wonderful, and that was surely going to change her life. For that whole day, and for the rest of the school holidays, she scarcely once put the mirror down. She even began taking it to bed, where she would sleep with her arms wrapped around Tiger, after taking one final, disbelieving look at his gigantic reflection in the mirror, and dream all night long that she could feel the warmth of a tiger's body – twice as big as her own – lying pressed up gently beside her, the sound and the throb of his purr sending her quickly into the deepest sleep she had ever known.

FOUR

Two years went by.

In that time, Claire grew used to the idea that the mirror was part of her life. She came to believe that she would never be able to find a way into the world that it reflected – the world that was so much brighter and more colourful and more glorious than her own. This was a disappointment to her, of course, but she reconciled herself to it. There was nothing else she could do, after all, and in the meantime she felt lucky to have the privilege and the pleasure (the secret pleasure) of being able to look into the mirror whenever she wanted. She kept it carefully wrapped in a piece of green velvet in the drawer of the table beside her bed.

Usually Claire would take the mirror with her whenever she and her parents went out. They grew used to seeing it, and didn't ask any questions when Claire would sit in the back of the car, for instance, gazing in private wonder at the vast, beautiful landscape reflected in the mirror as she turned it this way and that. Sometimes, in the earliest days, she might catch a glimpse of a unicorn running out shyly from between

the distant trees, or a griffin or even a flame-spouting dragon soaring through the skies overhead. Meanwhile she felt sorry for her mother and father, who looked out of their car window and could only see the grey and uniform buildings of their home town or the dull, unchanging contours of the motorway.

Very occasionally, she would even take the mirror to school. When she did this, what she saw reflected was a recognisable version of her own school, but with certain differences. In fact, as the years had gone by, she found that the nature of all the reflections in the mirror had been changing, although it was happening so slowly and subtly that she barely noticed it at first. Gradually, the sandcastle and all its magnificent grounds had started to fade and shift, and what replaced it were the familiar surroundings of her own house, the well-known shapes of her garden, but in each case somehow transformed, made more welcoming and delightful. This change in the reflections – the loss of her vibrant, colourful fantasy world – did not affect her profoundly: it felt perfectly natural to Claire, although it did leave her with a certain sense of melancholy. It was the same with her school buildings. The ones she saw in the mirror were clearly the same buildings, but there were differences: in the mirror, they seemed somehow cleaner, and brighter, and more spacious. The expressions on many of her teachers' faces were kinder and wiser. Her other classmates had a more lively glint in their eyes, more colour in their complexions, looked altogether happier and more healthy. These differences intrigued her, but still, Claire did not bring the mirror to school very often.

The town where she lived was called Kennoway, and right on the edge of it (a long way from Claire's house) was a district called The Dales. This was where Claire's best friend Aggie lived. Her full name was Agnieszka and her mum and dad were Polish. They had come from Poland a few years ago and lived in a few different places before settling down in The Dales, which had quite a distinctive feel to it, compared to the rest of the town. The houses were old and a bit run-down but Claire still liked them. They had more character than the modern ones on her own estate. The shops were older, too, and there weren't any of the supermarkets or chain stores you found in the main part of Kennoway. There were a couple of cafés and restaurants but they, too, had been there for years and were run by local families. Aggie liked living there as there were lots of other Polish families in the area, as well as Romanians, Indians, Pakistanis, Afro-Caribbeans and all sorts of other interesting people. Claire's parents told her it was a dangerous place and she should be extra careful when visiting, but she couldn't really see what they meant and always felt perfectly safe when she went there. Not that she and Aggie ever did anything really exciting. Usually they would buy some chocolate and something to drink from the newsagent on the corner of the street where Aggie lived, then walk over to a spot called the Village Square – probably because once, years ago, The Dales had been a separate village, not part of Kennoway itself. Like the rest of The

Dales, the Village Square was a bit shabby, but it had some nice shops and cafés on three sides, and a big stone fountain in the middle which sometimes worked. It was a good place to sit and chat, anyway.

Claire and Aggie would talk about all sorts of things, but one of their favourite topics was Amanda Gifford, the richest and most obnoxious girl at their school. Claire and Aggie had both disliked her from the very first day that they'd met. Her father ran a big construction company, and they lived in an enormous house with a swimming pool out in the countryside, way beyond the confines of the town. Every day she was driven to school by her chauffeur in a Range Rover that was so big it could barely fit down some of Kennoway's narrow roads, so that the smaller cars had to get out of the way and climb up onto the pavement. The windows of the car were tinted, which meant that Amanda could see out, but nobody could see in. In the back of the car, so the rumours went, were a TV set and a fridge full of fizzy drinks.

Most of the time Amanda ignored Claire. She had her own circle of friends, and they weren't interested in someone like her. But one summer, towards the very end of the school year, something happened which meant that they could no longer be merely indifferent to each other. Something happened which turned them into enemies.

It happened on Sports Day. This was a big, impressive occasion for which all of the teachers and most of the children's parents would turn up, if they could get time off work. Today Claire's mum was there and so was Amanda

Gifford's mother. She had arrived in the Range Rover and even Claire had to admit that she looked incredibly glamorous in her sleeveless top and tight denim skirt. She was probably about forty but she dressed – and looked – as if she was twenty-five.

Claire was only taking part in a couple of the races; she was not very good at athletics. But Aggie was one of the best runners in their year, especially over long distances. She was expected to win the 800 metres.

It was one of the last races to be run that day. Aggie had asked Claire to stand on the far side of the track, away from most of the spectators, so that she could cheer her on as she approached the last part of her final lap. As Claire made her way over there, she realised that she was being followed. She turned and saw that a boy called Peter Lewis was tagging along behind her. She sighed. Peter was a pain. He followed her everywhere and was always trying to persuade her to become friends with him. Why was he doing this now? He didn't have any special reason to stand on this side of the track, far from everybody else. He was only doing it because she was.

'Go away, Peter,' she said. 'I don't want you following me.'

'It's a free country, isn't it?' Peter insisted, in his whiny voice. 'I'll stand where I want to.'

'Fine,' said Claire, stomping off at a quicker pace. She couldn't stop him being there, but she wasn't going to talk to him.

The only other person standing on this side of the track

was Mr Drummond, the head teacher. Another person she didn't like! He was a cold, unfriendly man whose very presence seemed to cast a dark shadow over the school every day. This afternoon he nodded to her and said, 'Hello, Cathy,' which was typical. He never managed to remember who she was.

The race began. Amanda Gifford was also taking part. She was one of four or five girls who were almost as fast as Aggie. It was a very close thing. With only two hundred yards to go, there was almost nothing to choose between the four girls at the front. They were still running together in a tight bunch. And then there was a collision. From a distance, it just looked as if two of the girls had bumped into each other, but Claire saw the whole thing close up. She could see that Aggie had been pulling into the lead, when Amanda deliberately ran into her and pushed her off the track. Aggie had tripped and almost fallen over, and even though she recovered her balance and carried on running, she had lost precious seconds, and had no chance of winning the race after that. She came in fifth.

'Did you see that?' Claire asked, furious, turning to Mr Drummond. He stared at her with a blank look in his eyes, and said something like, 'Shocking,' but he didn't seem to mean it. In any case, Claire didn't wait to hear any more. Without stopping to ask Peter if he had also seen the incident, she ran at full speed back to the other side of the track. She quickly spotted Amanda Gifford (who had come second) and grabbed her by the shoulder.

'You pushed my friend!' she said. 'You stopped her from winning the race.'

'What are you talking about?' Amanda replied.

Afterwards, Claire found it hard to say exactly what happened next. Her memory smudged the events of the next few minutes into a blur. All she knew was that there was a fight, a terrible fight. By the time two of the teachers had pulled them apart, Claire had a livid, bloody scar down one side of her face, and Amanda was bleeding from her nose and her lip. Their mothers had rushed over and the other parents were staring at them both in silent amazement (secretly pleased that somebody else's children – not their own – had brought about this disgrace). Sports Day – one of the most keenly anticipated days in the school calendar – had been reduced to chaos.

Mr Drummond demanded to see both children first thing the next morning.

When she got to his office, Claire found that Peter Lewis was loitering outside.

'Not you again!' she said. 'What are you doing here?'

'I saw what happened yesterday,' Peter explained. 'I thought you might want me to come and back you up.'

Claire looked at him. It was nice of him to offer to help, she supposed, but there was something about Peter that really annoyed her. It was probably his horn-rimmed glasses, or the braces on his teeth, or his shrill little voice which always reminded her of fingernails being scraped along glass.

'No thank you,' she said.

'Well anyway, there's something you should know,' he said. 'I don't think Mr Drummond's going to believe you, because—'

But Claire had already stopped listening, and was knocking on the door of Mr Drummond's office.

The meeting was a disaster.

Claire accused Amanda of deliberately pushing her friend off the track. Amanda said that she had done no such thing. And then Mr Drummond, after listening to them accusing and insulting each other for a few noisy minutes, intervened and took Amanda's side.

'What you seem to forget, Cathy,' he pointed out, 'is that I was there. Standing right next to you. I saw the whole thing as well. And it's my considered opinion that nothing untoward took place.'

When she tried to protest he simply talked over her, and said that the way she had attacked Amanda was unforgivable. To add insult to injury, he suspended her from school for the rest of the week.

Claire left the office, her face burning red and her cheeks wet with tears. Peter was still standing outside.

'Are you OK?' he said, offering her a tissue.

She took the tissue and wiped the tears away.

'I did try to warn you,' he said.

'Warn me about what?'

'Mr Drummond and Amanda's father are mates,' he explained. 'They both sit on the town council, for one thing.

And every Saturday morning they play golf together. I've seen them.'

Claire stared at him. She didn't know what to say, and in the end just blurted out defiantly: 'Yeah, I knew that.'

But she hadn't known it, of course. That evening, she sat for a long time on her bed, thinking about this turn of events as she hugged Tiger close to her chest. The light was beginning to fade but she didn't turn her bedside lamp on. She sat there, thinking, until it was quite dark. She didn't even notice that night had fallen.

So, she thought, this is how the world really works. A girl had done something wrong, a girl had cheated, and her friend had suffered for it. And then, when Claire had tried to put things right, nobody had let her. She had been telling the truth, but a powerful man had contradicted her – had told a lie – for no other reason than because he wanted to keep on the right side of another powerful man. She had been so certain that he would believe the truth. Truth was the most important thing in life, wasn't it? She had always thought so. But apparently it wasn't. Not to some people.

She had never been more depressed in her life. As the black mood stole over her, she turned on her bedside lamp, took the fragment of mirror out of its drawer, and looked accusingly at its surface. It seemed more than usually smudged and dirty today. So dirty, in fact, that she could hardly see anything in it at all, apart from a very blurred and shadowy reflection of her own face. She angled the mirror so that she could see the face of Tiger, but the mirror didn't make him look at all like a real tiger tonight. Crossly, she pushed her toy out of bed onto the floor. Then she put the mirror away again, turned out the light, rolled over onto her side and stared for a long time into the darkness.

FIVE

Two more years went by, and in that time Claire left her primary school, which was a relief, as she had really started to hate Mr Drummond. After he had pretended not to believe her about the Sports Day story, she began to notice that he was like this all the time. He never tried to be fair and was never concerned about the truth. Every decision he made was based on self-interest. His only goals were to keep the boys and girls in line and consolidate his own power as headmaster. As a result he was feared, but not respected. In fact Claire was not the only person who hated him – not by any means.

When she went to a new secondary school, though, she somehow managed to get separated from Aggie, who went to a different one, closer to her house. And so gradually, as often happens, they drifted apart and stopped seeing each other.

Claire didn't like her new school much either. For one thing Amanda Gifford and Peter Lewis were still in her class: there seemed to be no getting rid of them. And she didn't manage to make a new best friend to replace Aggie. She became quite a solitary girl. Nobody really took much notice of her.

Oddly enough, the person who was most friendly to her, during this time, wasn't one of the other children at all, but one of the teachers. Mrs Daintry taught history and for some reason (perhaps simply because she was such a good teacher) this soon became Claire's favourite subject, and the one she was best at. The other children found it boring to think about the past. They were only interested in the present moment, and what was going to happen next in their own lives. But Mrs Daintry told them all once that history always repeats itself, and that one of the best ways of understanding what is happening now is to read about what's happened before, and Claire knew exactly what she meant. From then on, she found it fascinating to hear about the empires which had risen and fallen because of the arrogance of a handful of people, the great wars and battles which sometimes seemed to have been fought over nothing at all, the conflicts and crises which had been provoked down the ages because someone had been too greedy or too hungry for power. It seemed to her that the great theme of history was the search for justice, the struggle to ensure that everybody in the world was given a fair chance to do well and to make the most of their lives, but again and again things went wrong, people kept making the same mistakes, and the weak were not able to defend themselves because it was always the rich and powerful people who determined the course of events. Her mind kept going back to the Sports Day, two years ago, when she had tried to stand up for her friend and Mr Drummond wouldn't listen because he had his own goals to pursue. Claire realised that she had learned an important lesson that day and that she could learn the same lesson by looking at the never-ending roster of similar stories which made up human history: a history which seemed continuously to repeat itself in spiralling patterns.

*

One day in the holidays just before Christmas, much to her own surprise, Claire found herself sitting in the front room of Mrs Daintry's house, sipping tea and eating ginger biscuits. She'd been invited over for tea and had been expecting to find other children there, but she was the only one. The ostensible reason for the visit was so she could borrow a book about the rise of the Nazis (which was the period they were studying at the moment) but she was starting to suspect there was more to it than that, because Mrs Daintry kept changing the subject and asking much more personal questions.

'Are you happy at school, Claire?' she said at one point.

'Yes, I suppose so.'

'And what about home – is everything OK between your mum and dad?'

'I suppose so,' she said, again – although actually her parents had been arguing all the time recently, and she had begun to spend a lot of evenings alone in her bedroom to get away from them when they started yelling at each other.

'You're looking so thin, these days,' said Mrs Daintry. 'You are eating properly, aren't you? We don't want you becoming unwell.'

'I'm fine, really,' said Claire. The questions were making her uncomfortable and she was glad when half an hour had gone by and she felt she could leave without appearing too rude.

Before leaving she asked if she could use Mrs Daintry's toilet. Like all the other rooms in the house, it was clean and nicely decorated but there seemed to be something a bit sad about it. Apparently Mrs Daintry used to be married herself but then her husband had left her for a much younger and prettier woman and now she lived on her own. Here in the loo almost everything was immaculate – polished tiles, soap and hand towels arranged just so – which made it surprising to see something on the shelf by the window that didn't seem to belong there: a dirty old fragment of glass, which on closer inspection turned out to be a piece of broken mirror.

Now, it's a strange thing, but ever since the Sports Day incident, Claire had not looked at her own fragment of mirror once. If she thought about it at all, it seemed to belong to a different part of her life altogether, a much more childish one, when she used to play a silly game which involved pretending to see fairy-tale castles and tigers and eagles where in reality there was only her parents' house and an empty grey sky. That was all in the past, as far as she was concerned, and could never be brought back. She had no idea why Mrs Daintry should have a similar-looking piece of mirror in her otherwise-spotless bathroom, but when Claire picked it up and looked at it, she felt a powerful sense of familiarity. The surface was so dirty that she couldn't make out any reflections, but just the weight and feel of it in her hand was enough to fill her with nostalgia, and she suddenly felt a terrible longing to go back to her parents' house and take her own mirror out of its drawer and look into it again.

And so, after washing her hands, she said goodbye and thank you to Mrs Daintry as quickly as possible, and set off towards home at a rapid pace.

Before she got there, however, she had three different encounters.

The first one should have been nice, but was actually just a bit embarrassing and sad. Mrs Daintry lived in The Dales, and since her house was so close to Aggie's Claire couldn't resist walking that way. It was just getting dark, and golden lamplight was beginning to spill out from people's windows onto the pavements. Some of the houses in Aggie's street were in poor condition but not hers: it really stood out, because the door was painted a rich, dark red, it had a lovely shiny golden door-knocker and, beneath that, a Christmas wreath adorned with plastic red holly berries and all sorts of dangling golden ornaments. At the top of the door were two little panes of glass, and the soft, yellowish light she could glimpse through these and through the front windows of the house made her want to go inside and warm herself by the log fire she knew would be burning in the cosy front room. She thought about knocking on the door to say hello but she was too shy. So she turned round instead but, just as she was leaving, she saw Aggie herself coming down the street towards her. She had another girl with her, who was black and tall and very pretty.

'Claire?' said Aggie, looking amazed but giving her a big hug. 'What are you doing here? This is my friend Miriam.'

After that they talked for a few minutes in a really awkward and stumbling way. It was clear that Aggie and Miriam were going inside the house but they didn't want to invite Claire in with them. So they were soon saying their goodbyes and making vague promises to keep in touch. (The kind of promises you know are never going to be kept.) And then Claire was on her way home again.

As she passed through the centre of town and was walking down the main street, she saw a bunch of people from school coming towards her. And not just any bunch of people, but the coolest, most unfriendly bunch of all. Amanda Gifford wasn't with them, thankfully, but they were all friends of hers – including David Knightley, the tallest, most popular, best-looking boy in her whole year, who had never so much as glanced in her direction, let alone spoken to her. Claire felt her stomach twist into a tight knot of anxiety, and she went stiff with mortification as the group approached. She looked down and kept her eyes fixed on the pavement. As they brushed past her, she thought she had got away with it, thought she had survived the encounter without provoking any comment, but then she heard one of the girls say a horrible thing – 'Do you think there's a face somewhere beneath all that acne?' – and the others all laughed and chuckled meanly. Claire felt the blood rushing to her face. Her cheeks stung with the shame of it and she strode onwards, her shoulders hunched and her hoodie pulled as tightly around her as it would go.

As she reached the corner of the street, just outside one of the big banks, Claire had the third of her encounters. She heard a voice calling to her: 'Hey darling, what's the rush?' It was George, the homeless man who seemed to spend most of his life there, next to the row of cashpoint machines. Most people were afraid of George, because he had long hair and a huge grey beard and yellow teeth and a red face, all of which made him look a bit scary, but Claire had spoken to him a few times and found that there was actually nothing scary about him at all. Sometimes she stopped to chat with him for a few minutes and sometimes she even gave him some money or went into the supermarket next door to get him some biscuits or a chocolate bar, although she often felt that all he really wanted her to buy was another of the miniature whisky bottles which he always kept by his side. Today she ignored him, in any case, and hurried past. She didn't want to speak to him or to anyone else any more.

As usual, Claire's parents ignored her when she got home, and she did not take off her hoodie until she got upstairs to her bedroom. Then she opened her wardrobe, which had a mirror fixed to the inside of the door. She pulled off the hood and looked closely at her face. The girl had been right. Her skin was terrible. She was covered in horrible red spots, some of which had turned into scabs. Why was this happening to her? It had begun a few months ago and there seemed to be nothing she could do about it. Her mother told her it was 'all part of growing up', which was no help at all. It did not stop

her thinking that she was turning into the most hideous-looking person she had ever seen in her life.

And so now, frantically, she rummaged through the junk that had accumulated in her bedside drawer in search of the old broken mirror, and eventually she found it, her fingers closing on the scrap of green velvet cloth in which she had last wrapped it all that time ago. Sitting down on her bed, she unfolded the velvet and took out the jagged, star-shaped object. It was pretty dusty. She wiped it with her sleeve. Then she drew a deep, nervous breath, and looked into the mirror.

At first she did not look into it directly. She turned it at different angles and looked at various reflections of her bedroom. When she saw that these reflections were basically no different from what she could see every day, with her own eyes, she felt a tremor of disappointment, but also – in a strange way – a certain relief. So it *had* been nothing but her imagination, after all. It was just an ordinary mirror – and a very dirty and misshapen one, at that. How could she ever have believed otherwise? There was no such thing as magic. Everybody knew that!

Finally she turned the mirror so that it was pointing directly at her own face.

And this time it was different. The same grey-blue eyes stared back at her, but her face was not the same. There were no spots, none at all. Her skin was pale and creamy and quite unblemished. This was her own face, yes, but at the same time one that she hardly recognised. This face was beautiful.

SIX

Claire began to carry the mirror around with her again. She took it wherever she went. Not just because it seemed to show her own face the way she wanted it to be, but because in the glimpses it offered of all the other things around her, so many of them appeared to be somehow brightened and improved.

However, these were precisely what it offered: glimpses, nothing more. It made Claire wonder if her memory was deceiving her, because as far as she could recall, when she was younger and used to look into the mirror, she used to see clear, steady reflected images. But it wasn't like that any more. The reflections came and went very quickly. By turning the mirror this way and that, she could often make them come back, but only for a few seconds at a time. It was like trying to listen to a radio that was never quite tuned in properly.

One Saturday morning while her parents were out somewhere, Claire had an accident. She was washing up her breakfast things and she dropped a mug on the kitchen floor. It broke, so she looked around for some newspaper to wrap up the shattered pieces. The only thing she could find was the local paper, the *Kennoway Trumpet*, which was delivered free of charge every week and usually went straight into the recycling bin without anybody reading it. This morning, though, Claire's attention was caught by the picture on the front page. It was a picture of two people she recognised. She forgot about clearing up the mug and started reading the story instead.

The two people in the photograph were her old headmaster (and enemy) Mr Drummond, and Amanda Gifford's father Basil. They were standing on some big building site, shaking hands and grinning at the camera. 'Council Gives the All-Clear for New Development', the headline said.

Claire learned a number of things from this story, and suddenly realised, to her shame, that she had not been paying much attention to what had been going on around her in the last few years. For a start, it turned out that Mr Drummond was not headmaster of her old primary school any more – he had moved on from that, and was now the Mayor of Kennoway. This meant, as far as she could make out, that he was basically running the whole town. And he had big plans for it: plans that were going to disrupt a lot of people's lives, and which called for the heavy involvement of Amanda Gifford's dad, by the looks of things.

In this picture, Mr Drummond and Mr Gifford were standing in front of a famous building on the outskirts of town. It was the old chocolate factory, built by the Bellweather family more than a hundred years ago, a massive but beautiful red-brick building standing in hundreds of acres of lawned grounds. Claire had good reason to recognise this building, because it was where her father worked, and when she was younger she had visited it twice – once for a guided tour, and once for a party which had been given for all the workers' children.

Later that day she showed her father the newspaper and asked him what was going on.

'They're closing the factory down,' he said.

'Does this mean you haven't got a job any more?'

'Not really. They've sacked me – they've sacked all the workers. But they're going to employ us all again.'

'What's the point of that?'

'It means they don't have to give us things like pensions and health insurance any more. And we'll all have to work at the new factory, of course.'

'Where's that?'

'About twenty-five miles away.'

Claire had never really been interested in her dad's job before, but the more he talked about it, the more she wanted to know. He told her that the Bellweathers had been a staunchly Christian family and, when they started the factory more than a century ago, their idea had been mainly to make drinking chocolate, which they hoped would stop people drinking so much wine, beer and spirits. They had been true philanthropists, he said, who paid their workers properly, gave them a clean and safe environment to work in, built them houses with gardens and poured lots of money into other projects which benefited the town as a whole. But five years ago the factory had been bought up by a much bigger international company, and since then lots of things had changed. Now many of the workers had been laid off, most of the chocolate was manufactured overseas, and the old factory had been sold to Gifford Construction Ltd, who proposed to turn it into a luxury hotel and spa.

Claire decided that she would like to know more about the history of the Bellweather family, and that the obvious place to look for information was the old town library. She hadn't been there for about five years, but she knew how to find it easily enough.

At least, she thought she did. It took her fifteen minutes or so to walk to where the library used to be, and when she got there, all she could see was a shopping centre. There was a woman standing outside in a fluorescent jacket, collecting money for some charity or other, so Claire went over to her and said:

'Excuse me, I'm looking for the library. Didn't it use to be near here?'

The woman laughed. 'Have you got a time machine?'

'Pardon?' said Claire.

'You're in the right place. But you're about three years too late. The library isn't here any more. They closed it down to build this instead.'

Claire thanked the woman and walked on into the shopping mall. It was full of all the usual places: coffee shops and clothes shops and mobile-phone shops. People were drifting about from one shop to another, trying to find

ways of spending their money, all with a slightly glazed, lifeless look in their eyes. The only thing that seemed to be propelling them forwards, Claire thought, was an instinctive, irresistible impulse to buy stuff, eat stuff and drink stuff.

She walked to the only part of the mall that looked attractive, where there was an ornamental pool in the centre, with a fountain playing and a few artificial plants around the edges. She sat down on the edge of the pool and took the broken mirror out of her pocket – carefully, so that nobody would notice what she was doing. She sat with her back to the pool and angled the mirror so it was pointing towards a shop selling handbags and jewellery and other accessories. She looked closely into the mirror.

Reflected in the glass was a big, warm, softly lit space, the walls lined with books of every size and description. It was the library, all right, and just as she remembered it from all those years ago, except that this one looked even more welcoming and well-maintained. There were people sitting at desks and tables, looking through books and newspapers, reading magazines and using computers. For almost a minute the reflection gleamed brightly on the surface of the mirror, reminding Claire of the times she used to come here with her mother, filling her with a powerful sense of longing, an aching, impossible desire to walk into that library again, to pluck a book down from the shelves, to absorb the knowledge it contained, to pass an hour or two in that generous space where everyone was welcome, irrespective of whether they had money to spend. She stared more and more intently into the mirror, not caring now whether anybody was watching her or not, and then she let out a deep, regretful sigh as the vision slowly faded and was replaced by dull reality.

Once again Claire, who had been wrapped in the silent cocoon of her own imagination, became aware of the chatter of the shoppers as they drifted by, the soporific murmur of the background music as it oozed out of the mall's speaker system. Reluctantly, she rose to her feet and put the mirror away.

As she did so, Claire spotted someone on the other side of the mall, coming out of a coffee shop with a plastic cup in his hand. It was David Knightley. He didn't notice her.

Claire's heart skipped and fumbled, her stomach flipped as if she was plunging downward on a roller coaster, and without stopping to think, or to ask herself what she was doing, with her eyes fixed on the strong, solid outline of David's shoulders and the perfect cut of his jet-black hair, she began walking after him, and followed him at a few yards' distance for about ten minutes, until she lost sight of him in the crowd.

SEVEN

And that was how Claire's obsession began. She didn't intend for it to happen like that, and she certainly didn't intend for it to take over her life. But it did.

She found that she was thinking about David constantly. She found that she was spending most of her spare time trying to think of ways she might possibly meet him. She found that she was doing the most ridiculous, unlikely things, such as googling his name when she should have been doing her homework, or furtively checking his different profiles on social media, or even – on one especially horrendous, mortifying occasion – writing his name over and over on successive lines of her exercise book when she was supposed to be planning an English essay. She knew that she was being stupid, knew that she was wasting her time and embarrassing herself, but it made no difference. The worst thing about it was that he took no notice of her whatsoever. He didn't even seem to know that she existed.

Of course David already had a girlfriend, and of course it was Amanda Gifford. They had a favourite café where they used to meet in the centre of town, and Claire's need to see him became so pathetic that she started going there herself, and sitting at a table on her own just so that she could look at him while they sat there kissing and whispering sweet nothings to each other. It was torture, but better than the torture of not seeing him at all.

One day while she was doing this, Aggie came into the café. She was by herself this time, and didn't seem in any hurry to go anywhere, so she bought herself a hot chocolate and then sat down with Claire and they started talking. It was pretty weird at first, because they hadn't really spoken to each other for years, and the days of their close friendship at primary school seemed a long time ago. They were both in their mid-teens by now, after all. But before long the awkwardness went away and they were chatting together like old friends again. The only trouble was that Claire was finding it hard to concentrate. What Aggie had to say sounded interesting, but she couldn't take her eyes off David and Amanda on the other side of the café.

'We might be going back to Poland soon,' Aggie was saying.

'For a holiday? That's nice,' said Claire, still staring across at the other table.

'No, I mean to live.'

'Oh. OK,' said Claire. It was as if she hadn't heard.

'Mum and Dad used to like it here but they say the town's changing,' said Aggie.

'Really?' Claire's eyes narrowed as she saw David reach across the table and take Amanda's hand.

'Like, the other day,' said Aggie, 'my mum was on the bus, and she was talking with her friend Mrs Dobrzynski. They were talking in Polish.'

'Why?' Claire asked, absently. 'Is she Polish too?'

'With a name like that?' said Aggie, looking at her in disbelief. 'Of course she is.'

'Right,' said Claire.

'And then this guy who was sitting opposite them started shouting at them and asking them why they couldn't talk in English if they were living in England and if they didn't want to they should go back to their own country. It was really nasty. They were both so upset that they had to get off the bus.'

'Yeah, I see what you mean,' said Claire. David had brought Amanda's hand to his lips and was giving it the tenderest of kisses. She felt sick.

'I don't think they'll go through with it, though,' said Aggie. 'I mean, they know I'm really happy at school here and everything.'

'Sure, yeah,' said Claire, who could see now that David was getting up and leaving. She would so like to have followed him.

'It's just that Dad says this town has never been the same since Mr Drummond became Mayor. Haven't you noticed how things are changing?'

'Mm-hm,' said Claire, watching David leave through the front door of the café, and walk off along the street. When he had left, it was as if the sun had gone down.

'They're knocking down half the houses in The Dales and putting up new ones that hardly anyone can afford. There are policemen on the street everywhere all of a sudden. Our local hospital's closed down. The youth club isn't there any more. And people have started being really rude to... you know, foreigners. People like us.'

Once they had said goodbye and she was walking home, Claire felt guilty for not listening to Aggie properly. What she was talking about sounded important. As she had told herself a hundred times before, she should really stop obsessing over David and concentrate on all the other things that were going on, the way that everything in Kennoway seemed to be going in the wrong direction since Mr Drummond had taken control. Like the closing down of the Bellweather factory, and the fact that it now took her father an hour and a half to get to work every day...

Just then, however, something did happen which took her mind off David. She was walking down a quiet street when she saw George the homeless man sitting on the pavement. It was a wet afternoon, and he was sitting close to the side of the road where a large amount of muddy rainwater had pooled because of a blocked drain. As Claire approached, she was overtaken by a massive black four-wheel drive with tinted windows, which she recognised at once: it was Amanda's. She must have phoned her chauffeur from the café and he had come to pick her up. The enormous, petrol-guzzling car drove past her and then went straight through the pool of rain and threw a huge splash of it right over George, soaking him to the skin with filthy water. He jumped to his feet at once and ran after the car.

'Oi! Watch what you're doing!' he shouted.

The car had stopped at some traffic lights. One of the back windows slid down and Amanda's head popped out.

'Don't you dare talk to me,' she said.

'Look what you just did!'

'That's your fault,' she answered, 'for sitting by the side of the road all day doing nothing. Why don't you go out and get a job like everybody else?'

She wound up her window again, and a few seconds later the traffic lights changed and the car roared away, sending more splashes in its wake. George walked slowly back to his blanket, shaking out his sleeves and treading carefully as the water in his shoes made a damp sploshing sound. He sat down with a squelch and reached out for the whisky bottle which he always kept by his side. He took a long sip from the bottle and then put it down, with a sigh of quiet resignation.

'Here,' said Claire. She had her sports bag with her, and she handed George her swimming towel. 'Dry yourself down, and clean yourself up. You look a right old mess.'

He took the towel off her gratefully and spent a little while making himself dry, muttering all this time about the bad manners of some people he could mention. Then he handed the towel back to Claire and said, 'How do I look?'

Claire gazed at him appraisingly for quite a few seconds. To be honest, he looked terrible. His clothes and his hair were still wet, and were both in a dreadful state as usual. His

face seemed redder than ever. His eyes were glazed and tired. There were breadcrumbs and bits of cigarette ash stuck in his beard. He looked much too thin. It was impossible to guess how old he was. He could have been any age from about thirty to about sixty.

'You look fine, George,' said Claire. 'Here – see for yourself.'

She reached into her bag and handed him a mirror. And whether she meant to or not (Claire could never really be quite sure about this afterwards), instead of giving him the ordinary compact mirror she always carried with her to check her own appearance, she passed him the dirty old fragment of broken mirror, wrapped in green velvet. Before she could realise her mistake (if indeed it was a mistake), George had taken it from her hands and was looking at himself in it.

He did not seem especially surprised by what he saw there, but he looked at the reflection for a very long time – much longer than it would have taken just to check whether he'd cleaned himself up properly after the splash. He looked at the mirror carefully and intently, turning it slightly this way and that, and as he did this something seemed to happen to his eyes – which up until that point had been quite expressionless – as if someone had turned on a light behind them, or as if someone had walked into a room which had been dark for many years, and thrown open the curtains onto faint sunlight.

After he had stared into the mirror for a minute or two, George lifted his gaze and looked up at Claire. But he didn't say anything, at first.

'Are you all right, George?' said Claire. And then, when he still didn't speak, she asked quietly, 'What did you see in there?'

George paused, and took a deep breath, as if it cost him a great effort to start answering her question.

'A few years ago,' he began, slowly and brokenly, 'I didn't use to live like this. I had a wife and a family, and we lived in another town, hundreds of miles from here. I had my own business and we were doing all right. Not rich or anything like that, but very comfortable. Then things started to go wrong. People stopped buying what I wanted to sell, and I needed to borrow more money from the banks, and suddenly they didn't want to lend money to people like me any more. I started losing money and I couldn't keep up the payments on the house and all the worry was making me angry and miserable. My wife stood by me but it was no use, I started to behave horribly towards her and instead of staying in and talking things over with her I went out every night and got drunk. When she and the children left me I hardly noticed at first...'

He paused and looked at Claire earnestly.

'I'm not blaming anyone, you understand. I behaved badly. Stupidly. Still, I shouldn't have ended up like this. But people fall through the cracks, you see. They fall through the cracks.'

He raised the mirror again and looked into it one more time.

'What do I see? Is that what you wanted to know? I see my own face, of course. But not the way it really is. I know I look pretty wrecked, in real life. But in here, I just see the face of an ordinary middle-aged man. And I'm not sitting on this blanket, either, soaked to the skin. I'm in somebody's house. I don't think I've ever seen it before, but I think somehow it's my own house. Maybe it's the house I would have gone on to buy for us all once the children had got a bit bigger. And I'm not alone in the house. Not like I am here. No, my wife is there, and my children are there, both of them. They're a bit more grown up now, but I can recognise them all right. We're all sitting around the dinner table, and the children have just lit two candles, and there's a nice warm fire burning in the hearth, and my wife is just bringing something to the table, something good to eat.'

George took one final, long, yearning look into the mirror. 'Beautiful,' he whispered to himself. 'It all looks so beautiful.' Then his eyes went blank and dark again, as if someone had drawn the curtains on the room once more. And all he said to Claire, as he handed back the mirror, was:

'I must be drunker than I thought.'

EIGHT

The sign appeared one morning quite suddenly, and quite unexpectedly, on the side of the hill that rose up at the back of Claire's house on the western edge of the town.

It was a massive wooden sign, supported on two great poles. It was so big that it even blocked out some of the sunlight.

It consisted of a picture, and a slogan. The picture showed the stern, resolute face of Mr Drummond, and behind him, much smaller, an image of the town itself – or at least, the town as he wanted it to become. The slogan said: 'Thomas Drummond – The Man Who Puts Kennoway First'.

Because of its size, and its position on the hill, the sign loomed above the whole town, and cast a shadow over it. You could never forget that it was there.

And yes, the town itself was changing rapidly, in accordance with the vision expressed in the picture. Older houses were being demolished. More and bigger roads were being built, and the air was clogging up with fumes from cars like Amanda's. New buildings were springing up everywhere, all accompanied by hoardings with the name Gifford Construction Ltd on them. A big new police station had been built, and a big new prison, because Mr Drummond was adamant that Kennoway was beset by crime, and the only solution was to lock up more and more of its citizens. Bigger still were the new town hall, council offices and Mayor's residence that he was building in order to reflect the importance of his own position. In addition, he boasted of creating more jobs by setting up a new private security service to work side by side with the police in order to protect his staff and (in particular) himself, so that now, wherever you were in Kennoway, you never seemed to be far from some man in uniform who would stare at you accusingly until you moved on and went away.

All of these projects cost money, of course. But money always seemed to be available for them, even though Mr Drummond and his council were constantly shutting down schools, libraries, clinics, care homes and other useful institutions because they claimed they didn't have enough money to pay for them.

As for that slogan about putting 'Kennoway First', this was a phrase Mr Drummond had invented in one of his speeches and which had proved so popular that he had taken to repeating it again and again. It started appearing on signs and posters on every square and every street as well. Until recently, Kennoway had been twinned with a city in the South of France but one of the first things Mr Drummond did after becoming Mayor was to cancel that arrangement, saying that it cost too much and produced no benefits. For too long, he insisted, the town had been wasting money on silly schemes like this instead of spending it on its own citizens. From now on, he said, people from Kennoway should have the first choice of jobs and be first in the queue for the hospital. There were too many foreigners here anyway. The ones who already lived here could stay if they wanted to, but it wasn't practical to let any more in. The town was full, and for too long now, the local people had been taken advantage of and made to look like fools. It was true – he admitted – that some of the foreigners did useful jobs. Many of the men worked as builders for Gifford Construction, and their wives worked as cleaners or cooks for some of the town's wealthier families. But the fact of the matter was, these people didn't really belong here. From now on, it was going to be KENNOWAY FIRST.

Claire didn't really agree with any of this but she noticed that quite a few people did, and because a powerful and respectable man like Mr Drummond had started to say these things, many other people who might have kept their opinions to themselves were now emboldened to express them openly. The atmosphere in the town became increasingly bitter and divided. There were reports of Poles, Romanians and others being attacked in the street, and one day...

One day, Claire read a report in the newspaper and as soon as she saw it she felt sick and ran down to The Dales as fast as she could.

She reached Aggie's house and found that the story was true.

The windows had been smashed in and were now boarded up. The front door had been vandalised and horrible, cruel slogans had been daubed all over it, along with a Nazi symbol. The slogans were written in brown letters and Claire realised that the people who had done this hadn't used paint at all, but human waste.

As she stood there, staring, her eyes filling with tears, a woman came out of the house next door and stood beside her.

'They were such nice people,' Claire heard herself saying, in a trembling voice. 'They never hurt anybody.'

'I know – shocking, isn't it?' the woman said. 'They've gone now. Back to Warsaw. Two days ago. Didn't want to stay here any more, and I don't blame them.'

She squeezed Claire's shoulder and went back inside.

Slowly, then, Claire took the broken mirror from the pocket of her hoodie. She turned round so that she had her back to the door, and held the mirror away from her, her arm outstretched, so that the whole door was reflected in it.

What she saw almost broke her heart. The reflection took her straight back to that Christmas, a few years ago, when she had stood on the steps outside Aggie's parents' house, bathed in the soft yellow light that spilled from their windows. The door, once again, was a rich, dark red, with its shiny door-knocker and its jolly, festive Christmas wreath, adorned with red holly berries and hanging golden ornaments. It looked so friendly, so welcoming, such a plain and potent symbol of the values of a good, kind, generous family, that Claire forgot she was actually standing outside their house on a late-summer

evening, that the windows had been smashed in and the door defaced, that Aggie and her family had left the town in disgust and would never be coming back.

Slowly, like a sleepwalker, she moved away from the house with steady, trancelike steps. Her eyes never left the mirror, but she raised it up so that, instead of the old front door, it now reflected her own face. As always when she looked in this mirror, the face it showed her was a beautiful one, with delicate features, perfect skin and bright, intelligent eyes. In fact – as anyone could have told her – it was no different, these days, to Claire's real face, the one she presented to the world all the time But she had not come to realise that yet. To her, the images reflected by the mirror still represented her longings, the things that could not possibly come true, and so she was scarcely surprised when, behind the reflection of her face, she gradually discerned the outline of a boy approaching, walking behind her, catching up with her in the street. As he came closer, she knew with a dawning, glorious certainty who it was going to be: those broad, powerful shoulders, that immaculate jet-black hair... It was David. And she knew, too, that their moment had finally come, and that he was going to speak to her at last.

'Claire?' said the voice behind her. 'What are you doing here?'

She turned.

She turned and smiled.

But it wasn't David.

It was Peter Lewis, of all people.

NINE

Claire was so startled when she saw him that she dropped the mirror onto the pavement. For a horrible moment she thought that it had broken. When Peter bent down to pick it up and handed it back to her, she was relieved to see that it was still in one piece, but hated the thought of him touching it and snatched it from him rudely.

'That's mine, thank you,' she said, slipping it into her pocket as quickly as she could. She was annoyed to see that, even in those few seconds, Peter's eyes had been drawn to the dirty, broken old thing and he had taken a good look at it. What on earth must he think of her?

'Terrible about Aggie's house, isn't it?' he said.

Claire nodded.

'Where were you going now?'

'Back into town.'

'Do you mind if I walk with you for a while?'

'All right,' she said.

Claire looked properly at Peter, now, for the first time. Not just for the first time that day, but for the first time in about four years. They were no longer in the same class at school, and he had long since given up following her around forlornly like a loyal puppy, so she had not had cause to take any notice of him for a good while. And while he still wasn't as good-looking as David Knightley (nowhere near), he had certainly improved quite a lot over the years. He still wore horn-rimmed glasses, but he no longer had braces on his teeth, and his face wore a warm, good-natured, intelligent expression. His smile was especially nice. Claire's irritation faded and she found herself starting to feel quite glad that they had chanced upon each other in this way.

They walked back to the centre of the town, heading for Claire's usual café. Amanda and David were there too, as always, but this time Claire didn't find their presence at all distracting. She and Peter found a table on the other side of the room and simply ignored them, although a few minutes later when they got up to leave Claire couldn't resist saying:

'Ah well, there they go – the beautiful people.'

Peter merely snorted and said, unexpectedly, 'You're worth a hundred of them,' and Claire felt herself blushing.

They chatted for about thirty minutes. It was quite stilted and awkward at first, but Claire soon realised that Peter was so easy to talk to, and was so much more interesting than she'd expected, that she was quite disappointed when he took the last few sips of his drink and said:

'Look, I can't stay much longer. My mum and dad will be wondering where I am.'

'So will mine, I suppose,' said Claire.

'So the big question is –' Peter paused, and took a breath: 'Can I see you again?'

Claire felt her heart flutter and dive. 'Well,' she said, playing for time, 'you'll see me at school on Monday.'

'But tomorrow's Sunday,' said Peter. 'What about tomorrow?'

'OK,' said Claire, perhaps a little too quickly. 'Where shall we go?'

This was brilliant. She was going to go out on her very first date! But suddenly Peter asked an unexpected question:

'When you were little,' he said, 'did you ever go to that big dump that's at the back of your house?'

Claire had no idea why he was changing the subject like this.

'Yes…' she said, slowly, making no attempt to hide her puzzlement. All the while, what she was really thinking about was where Peter might take her tomorrow. Ice-skating perhaps? Or to the cinema? Yes, that's what she would prefer, definitely: the cinema. She hadn't been to the cinema for ages…

'Well,' said Peter, 'let's meet there.'

It took a moment for Claire to be sure that she had not misheard him. 'You mean… at the dump?'

'That's right. At the dump. Is that OK?'

She was too shocked to do anything but nod her agreement.

Afterwards, back at home with her parents, Claire grew angry – not just with Peter, for suggesting such a ridiculous meeting place, but with herself, for agreeing to join him there. What sort of weirdo thought that the local dump was a suitable venue for a date? And what sort of idiot went on a date with someone like that in the first place? It was obviously going to be a disaster, and the occasion she had been looking forward to with such excitement was now something she had started to dread.

*

Three o'clock on Sunday afternoon found her standing on the other side of the bushes at the top of the steep slope which led down to the dump. She felt absolutely stupid standing there in her grey hoodie, on a dull and cloudy afternoon, waiting for Peter to appear. And after she had been waiting about ten minutes, a horrible thought occurred to her: supposing he *wasn't* going to appear? Supposing he was playing some sort of nasty joke on her instead?

But then, as soon as she'd had this thought, she spotted him walking breathlessly along the ridge towards her.

'Hi,' he said. 'Sorry I'm late. Lunch went on a bit today.'

'That's OK,' said Claire.

They didn't kiss or anything like that – not even on the cheek. They just stood there for a moment or two, both a bit embarrassed and not sure what to do next.

After a while Peter sat down on the patchy grass. Claire sat down beside him.

'You're probably thinking this was a really strange place to meet,' he said.

'Pretty strange, yes,' Claire agreed.

'Well – there is a reason,' said Peter. Then he asked: 'You know that mirror you had with you yesterday? I don't suppose you've brought it with you?'

Claire reached instinctively for the pocket where she usually carried the mirror, but stopped before her hands closed on it. She was starting to feel suspicious again. Was Peter trying to make fun of her, in some peculiar way?

'Why do you want to know?'

'I don't know... I just had this idea – this feeling' (he was speaking slowly, finding the words with difficulty) 'that maybe it was here – on this dump – that you found it.'

Now Claire took the mirror out of her pocket.

'That's right. It was,' she said, wonderingly. 'How did you know?'

By way of reply, Peter reached into the pocket of his own anorak, and took out the very last thing that Claire had been expecting to see: a jagged, broken, dirty fragment of mirror just like her own. It shimmered and glittered in his hand as he talked to her, reflecting a sky much bluer than the one above their heads, which was still covered with dark grey clouds.

'I came here too, one day, when I was about... seven years old, I suppose,' he said. 'And this was what I found.'

After a few seconds' astonished silence, Claire held out her hand: 'Can I see?' she asked.

It was uncanny, holding Peter's mirror in her hand and looking into it to glimpse the subtly different, slightly brighter and warmer reflections it gave off as she tried it

out in various directions. It felt just like looking into her own mirror.

'Here,' Peter said, as he took it back from her. 'Can I borrow yours for a minute? There was something I wanted to try.'

Peter took both fragments of mirror in his hand. He looked at them carefully for a little while, then rotated Claire's mirror slightly and finally slid them both together.

The two fragments fitted together perfectly, like two pieces of a jigsaw puzzle.

Peter looked at Claire and smiled. She smiled back. She had never felt happier.

'Come on then,' he said. 'Let's go to the cinema or something.'

TEN

But in fact they did not go to the cinema. They started walking in that direction, but found they had so much to talk about that all they ended up doing was walking and talking.

To start with, they swapped stories about the things they had seen in their mirrors. They both agreed that the reflections had changed as they had grown older. Like Claire, Peter had begun by seeing magical, amazing but impossible images: as a young boy, he had been obsessed by dinosaurs, and at first the mirror had transformed his parents' house into a vast, elaborate cave, in which he had often glimpsed huge prehistoric lizards roaming amongst the fantastic rock formations and grotesque, enormous sculptures made up of stalagmites and stalagtites, gleaming with the moisture of underground rivers and waterfalls. But – like Claire's wonderful sandstone castle – these images had slowly started to fade and as the years went by had been replaced by less fantastic ones: reflections of the world around him which none the less always offered some sort of subtle, indefinable improvement upon everyday reality.

Claire told him about some of the things she had seen in her mirror recently: the old library which was now a shopping centre, and Homeless George's vision of his family dinner table. 'But the annoying thing is,' she said, 'that you only ever see these things in little pieces.'

'Well, I've been thinking about that,' said Peter. 'Supposing… supposing we're not the only ones who have them?'

'What do you mean?'

Instead of answering her directly, Peter said something mysterious. He asked her if she was doing anything next weekend, and if she thought she could get away from home for the whole of Saturday night. Claire wasn't at all sure what he had in mind. How well did she know this person, how far should she trust him? At the moment (and this in itself was rather frightening) she thought she would do almost anything that he asked her to…

'I suppose I could get away,' she said doubtfully. 'I could tell Mum that I was having a sleepover or something.'

'Could you?' said Peter. 'That would be brilliant.'

'But what's this all about?'

'I'll tell you next week,' said Peter. 'But please – promise me that you'll come. We need you. We won't be able to do it without you.'

*

Next Saturday evening, at about eight o'clock, Claire met Peter at the end of her street. He had a rucksack with him, and together they set off in the direction of the big hill which rose up behind her house and overlooked the whole of the town.

As they walked there and began climbing the hill itself, Claire noticed that there seemed to be quite a few other people headed in the same direction. At first they just found themselves walking alongside a few lone stragglers or small groups of pedestrians; but by the time they were halfway up the hill, the numbers had swelled until it was something like a throng. There were men and women of every age, children and pensioners, couples and family groups and people on their own. All seemed to be going the same way: towards the enormous ugly sign which the Mayor had raised up on the hill so that it looked down over the whole of Kennoway.

When they reached the sign, Claire found that a large crowd had gathered beneath it. People were sitting on the grass, sometimes talking to each other but mainly waiting in silence and looking quite serious. Many of them seemed to have brought food, but instead of eating by themselves, they were taking it over to a number of large trestle tables which had been set up on one side of the crowd. Peter went over to one of these tables and from his rucksack took out sandwiches and fruit, salads and cheese. 'Thank you,' said the woman behind the table. 'Help yourself to anything that's here. The idea is that everybody pitches in and shares.'

Peter and Claire took their paper plates of food and sat down on the grass next to a woman they both recognised: it was Mrs Daintry, who had once been their history teacher.

'Hello,' she said, 'I knew that you two would be coming.' She reached inside her handbag and brought out her fragment of broken mirror. 'Did you bring yours?' she asked. 'Of course you did. You take them everywhere with you, don't you? Just like the rest of us.'

Peter and Claire took out their mirrors, and laid them on the ground next to Mrs Daintry's. The evening light was fading and the final rays of the setting sun danced off the glass and sent dazzling shafts of light in every direction. All around them, people were doing the same.

'What's going on?' Claire asked. 'What are we here for?'

Mrs Daintry explained that it was time to try an experiment. All the people who possessed one of these mirrors had been blessed with a precious gift; a gift which allowed them some fleeting vision of how the world might look if it was a better place. Now it was time to try combining these gifts to see if, together, they could create a reflection that was bigger, more powerful and more lasting than the glimpses their owners had been able to catch by themselves.

'We will have to work in the dark,' Mrs Daintry said. 'But it won't be difficult. Not really. You just have to remember two things. You have to remember to *THINK HARD AND WORK TOGETHER*.'

And those were the words which Claire, and all the other people who had gathered on that hillside, tried to keep in their heads as they carried out their task all through the night. The sun went down and a full moon rose, and together they pulled down the sign until it lay flat on the ground. Then, working by

the light of the moon (and sometimes by the light of the torches on their mobile phones), they started arranging their fragments of mirror on the surface of the sign, fitting one against the other, piecing the fragments together as though they were parts of a massive jigsaw puzzle, trying to blend them into one, seamless whole. '*THINK HARD AND WORK TOGETHER,*' they kept repeating to themselves, as they gradually put the new, enormous mirror into place, piece by piece, so that, by the time it was finished – just before dawn – it covered the entire hoarding, from top to bottom and from side to side.

After that they used ropes and pulleys to raise the sign into an upright position once again, and there the mirror stood. The light of the moon shimmered back from its flawless surface.

Then they sat down together on the side of the hill, and waited for the sun to rise.

They waited to see what the mirror would show them. They waited to see if it would show them how to make their town a better place to live.

Slowly, from behind the crest of the hill, the first rays of sunlight started to appear.

And gradually, as the sky became lighter and lighter, the image reflected by the mirror started to take shape, to become clearer and more distinct. The details started to emerge, one by one. And the crowd watched in silent wonder as the giant mirror revealed to them a vision of their town, their world, that was in every way better and more beautiful than the one they had for so long been used to.

When the vision was complete, they continued to stare at it in silence. Nobody said anything for a long time.

*

What had they seen in the mirror?

That's for you to decide.